Lee Bennett Hopkins

MOTHER GOOSE AND HER Children

Sadlier-Oxford

A Division of William H. Sadlier, Inc.

Dear Girls and Boys,

I was your age when I first met Little Boy Blue and Jumping Joan. Now I'd like you to meet them. You don't have far to go. Just turn the page and enter the world of **Mother Goose and Her Children**.

Come with me and we'll recite our ABCs, chant a few rhymes, and sing a song or two. Maybe we'll be able to wake up Little Boy Blue.

Happy Poetry-ing!

Lee Bennett Hopkins

Contents

ABC Song

A, B, C, D, E, F, G,
H, I, J, K, L-M-N-O-P,
Q, R, S and T, U, V,
W, X and Y and Z.
Now I know my ABC's,
Next time won't you sing with me?

LITTLE BOY BLUE

Little Boy Blue,
Come blow your horn;
The sheep's in the meadow,
The cow's in the corn.
Where is the boy
Who looks after the sheep?
He's under a haystack
Fast asleep.

Will you wake him?
No, not I,
For if I do,
He's sure to cry.

Betty Botter

Betty Botter bought some butter,
But, she said, the butter's bitter.
If I put it in my batter,
It will make my batter bitter.
But a bit of better butter
Will make my batter better.
So she bought a bit of butter
Better than her bitter butter,
And she put it in her batter
And the batter was not bitter.
So 'twas better Betty Botter
Bought a bit of better butter.

Little Jumping Joan

Here am I,
Little Jumping Joan;
When nobody's with me
I am always alone.

Jack, Be Nimble

Jack, be nimble.

Jack, be quick.

Jack, jump over the candlestick.

Rain, Rain, Go Away

Rain,

Rain,

Go away;

Come again

Another day.

Little Suzy

Wants to play.

JOHNNY SHALL RIDE

Ride away, ride away,
Johnny shall ride;
He shall have a pussy cat
Tied to one side.
He shall have a little dog
Tied to the other,
And Johnny shall ride
To see his grandmother.

15

Sleep, Baby, Sleep

Sleep, baby, sleep.
Father guards the sheep.
Mother shakes the
    dreamland tree
And from it falls
Sweet dreams for thee.

Sleep, baby, sleep.